The Thing I Say I Saw Last Night

A Christmas Story

written by Wendy McKernan
illustrated by Izabela Bzymek

 **Little Dragon Publishing**
www.littledragonpublishing.com
Vancouver, Canada

The Thing I Say I Saw Last Night: A Christmas Story
first published in Canada in 2011 by Little Dragon Publishing.
www.littledragonpublishing.com

Little Dragon Publishing

Library and Archives Canada Cataloguing in Publication

McKernan, Wendy, 1967-
The thing I say I saw last night : a Christmas story / written by Wendy
McKernan ; illustrated by Izabela Bzymek.

ISBN 978-0-9866204-0-9 (bound).--ISBN 978-0-9866204-1-6 (pbk.)

1. Christmas stories, Canadian (English). I. Bzymek, Izabela, 1979- II. Title.

PS8625.K47T55 2011   jC813'.6   C2010-905984-0

Book design by Izabela Bzymek and Wendy McKernan

This book is proudly printed and bound in Canada on FSC certified paper
which is acid-free and ancient-forest-friendly and has been processed chlorine-free.

Manufactured by Friesens Corporation
in Altona, MB, Canada October, 2010 Job # 59803

To Linderella for her endless enthusiasm,
encouragement and support.
xox Wendy

For my two wonderful nephews,
Damian and Dominik.
Love your auntie Iza

Wake up, little sister, and make your dreams leave.
For something has happened, you'll never believe.

But my tale's much better than a boring old dream.
And the moral of this story? Things aren't as they seem!

The beginning you know,
it's the same every night.
I put on my pj's
and turn out the light.

Mother comes in to wish me good night.
She talks about bed bugs, and warns me—
they bite!

Last night was no different— 'twas the same as before.
She blew me a kiss as she half-closed my door.

I lay cozy in bed,
tucked in nice and tight,
when I heard a strange noise
and had quite a fright.

What was the noise?
You didn't say.
Quick, tell me now.
Why the delay?

I first heard a crash, next a bang and a boom.
Then I heard footsteps right next to my room.
Felt a chill up my spine as a shadow drew near.
Whatever was coming, it soon would be here.

What happened then?
Did it wail or shriek?
Did you hide in the closet?
Did you take a peek?

I gathered my gear,
to swing into action;
cracked open the door,
but only a fraction!

You got out of bed?
How did you dare?
Then did you see it?
Was something there?

I just caught
a glimpse.
But oh, what
a sight!

The
THING
I say
I saw
last
night.

What was the colour?
Was it **purple** and HAIRY?
And when you saw it—
did it look scary?

I couldn't see the colour, the lighting was dim. But one thing I noticed, it sure wasn't **slim!**

As it turned down the hall, I saw a **HUMP** on its back.

It left **huge**, wet footprints,
so I followed its track.

From under its hat
grew a shock of white hair.
It gave me a wink,
then was no longer there.

What happened next?
Did the creature escape?
Did it climb out the window?
What was its fate?

The thing was no creature, no monster, no brute.
It was dressed quite smartly, and wearing a suit.

I crept down the stairs,

one

step

at a

time.

There stood the intruder – committing no crime.

His cheeks were quite rosy, as red as his suit. The hump on his back? A sack full of loot!

His hair and his beard were as white as the snow.
His laughter? His greeting?
"MERRY CHRISTMAS! HO, HO, HO!"

Who would have guessed it? Who would have thought? That late last night,

St. Nick would get caught!